W9-BBX-834

Read to Me, Grandpa

Read to Me, Grandpa

EDITED BY GLORYA HALE

JELLYBEAN PRESS
NEW YORK • AVENEL, NEW JERSEY

Introduction and Compilation
Copyright © 1993 by Outlet Book Company, Inc.

First published in 1993 by JellyBean Press,
distributed by Outlet Book Company, Inc.,
a Random House Company,
40 Engelhard Avenue
Avenel, New Jersey 07001

Designed by Liz Trovato

Manufactured in the United States

Library of Congress Cataloging-in-Publication Data

Read to Me Grandpa / edited by Glorya Hale ; illustrated
by Jesse Willcox Smith and Charles Robinson.
p. cm.
Summary : an illustrated collection of fairy tales, fables,
and poems by such authors as Robert Louis Stevenson and
Henry Longfellow.
1. Children's literature. [1. Literature—Collections.]
I. Hale, Glorya II. Smith, Jesse Willcox, ill.
III. Robinson, Charles, 1931- ill.
PZ5.R19844 1993
808.8'99282—dc20
93-7320
CIP
AC

ISBN: 0-517-09349-9

8 7 6 5 4 3 2 1

CONTENTS

INTRODUCTION

A small hand slips into yours and a piping voice says, "Please read to me, Grandpa."

"But what shall I read?" you might ask.

"A story or poem you liked when you were a boy," the child might reply.

Read to Me, Grandpa is a delightful collection of stories, fables, and poems from your own childhood that you can now enjoy again with the youngest generation. Surely you can remember the delicious tremor of excitement when you first heard the giant, in "Jack the Giant-Killer," roar "Fe fi fo fum, I smell the blood of an Englishman." Undoubtedly, you can recall the sympathy you felt for Hans Christian Andersen's poor ugly duckling, and how you laughed at the antics of the clever Puss in Boots who changed the fortunes of the miller's son. Here, too, are three familiar stories by the Brothers Grimm—"Rumpelstiltskin," "The Frog Prince," and "Hansel and Gretel."

Also included are some of Aesop's best fables, a selection of poems from *A Child's Garden of Verses* by Robert Louis Stevenson, and two marvelous poems by Henry Wadsworth Longfellow—*Paul Revere's Ride* and *The Children's Hour.*

This beautifully designed book, with its charming illustrations by such well-known artists as Jessie Willcox Smith, Anne Anderson, and Margaret W. Tarrant, will surely reawaken memories of your own childhood, of the pleasures of learning to read and of being read to. And together you and the children who are very special to you can visit enchanted lands—of giants and ogres, of princes and princesses, of magic spells and wondrous imaginings—and share moments that will become their golden memories.

GLORYA HALE

Jack the Giant-Killer

ONCE upon a time, in a cave on the top of a mountain in Cornwall, in England, there lived a giant named Cormoran. If three tall men stood one on top of another, they would be the height of this giant. He was so fat, too, that it would take some time to walk around him.

At the foot of this mountain where the giant lived there were several farms. When the giant wanted a meal, he strode down the hillside and robbed the farmers. Sometimes he carried off half a dozen oxen and a dozen sheep at a time. The oxen he slung over his shoulders and the sheep he tied around his waist.

The poor farmers were almost ruined, when a brave boy, called Jack, the son of one of them, determined to put an end to the giant's visits.

One dark night, Jack dug a pit at the foot of the mountain. Across the mouth of the pit he laid sticks, and mud, and straw, until no one could know there was a pit beneath. Early the next morning, Jack blew his cowhorn loudly and the giant woke with a start.

"Who is disturbing me at this time of day?" he asked, and, dressing quickly, he strode down the mountainside. At the foot of the mountain, on a big stone, sat Jack.

ELIZABETH CURTIS

"It was you who woke me, was it?" roared the giant, catching sight of the farmer's son. "Well, you shall pay for it," and he dashed forward. But the earth gave way beneath him and in a moment he was lying at the bottom of the pit.

Jack came to the edge of the pit, sat down, and laughed at the despair of the giant, who slowly picked himself up. When he stood on tiptoe, only his head appeared above the pit. This was Jack's chance. He seized his axe and with one blow struck off the giant's head.

Soon all around the countryside it was known how clever and brave Jack had been. The people were all very proud of him and gave him a sword and a belt. On the belt was embroidered, in letters of gold:

This is the valiant Cornishman

Who slew the giant Cormoran.

And this is how Jack got the name Jack the Giant-Killer.

After this adventure, Jack made up his mind to kill as many wicked giants as he could.

One day, a few weeks later, Jack set out on his travels. Late that afternoon he reached a forest. Through the trees he spied a castle. He asked to whom it belonged, and was told that the giant Blunderbore owned it and was living in it. This was good news for Jack, but since he was tired he sat down to rest before going to the castle. He was trying to plan an attack upon the giant when he fell fast asleep.

Jack had not been asleep very long when Blunderbore came by. Since he had just had dinner he might have passed the sleeping boy, but he noticed the writing on his belt.

"This is the valiant Cornishman

Who slew the giant Cormoran,"

read Blunderbore. "Ha-ha!" he said, as he picked Jack up and put him in his pocket.

When Jack woke, and found himself there, he was so terrified that he shook from top to toe. When the giant felt him tremble, he knew he was awake.

"Ha-ha, he-he, ho-ho! So you killed my brother Cormoran, did you? Now I'll kill you. Ha-ha, he-he, ho-ho!" And the giant laughed so loudly that Jack felt as if he were in the middle of an earthquake.

When they reached the castle, Blunderbore locked Jack in an upstairs room. Then he went off to fetch another giant who lived in the same forest. Left alone, Jack looked around the room, determined to find some way of escape. But he could not. However, in one corner of the room there was a bundle of rope. An idea struck Jack. He unrolled the rope and made two slip knots. Then he stood at the window and watched.

At last he saw what he was waiting for. The two giants were coming along slowly, arm in arm. The path along which they walked passed close under Jack's window.

As they drew near, Jack heard Blunderbore say, "I found a plump lad in the forest this morning. We'll have him for breakfast tomorrow."

Will you indeed? thought Jack, and at that moment the two giants were beneath his window. Jack, quick as lightning, flung down the rope with its slip knots. One knot passed over the head of Blunderbore, and one over the head of his friend. Jack pulled with might and main and in two minutes both giants were strangled.

Then Jack let himself down from the window by the remainder of the rope. He took the keys from Blunderbore's pockets and unlocked the doors of the rooms where many knights and ladies were imprisoned. As he opened each door he made a low bow, and said, "My lords and ladies, the castle is now yours." Then he went on his way.

After Jack passed through the forest and climbed over a mountain he found himself in a lonely valley. He was hoping a cottage was near, where he might rest for the night, when, turning a corner, he found himself in front of a castle. He was too tired to go farther so he knocked at the door. It was opened by a giant with two heads.

When Jack saw this two-headed giant he remembered he had heard that he was the owner of four valuable things—a wonderful coat, a remarkable cap, an amazing sword, and a fantastic pair of shoes. The coat made the wearer invisible. The cap told him whatever he wanted to know. The sword could cut through anything. The shoes could rush as quickly as the wind. Jack made up his mind to get them.

"It is worthwhile risking a good deal to possess these marvelous things," said Jack to himself. Jack told the giant that he was a traveler who had lost his way.

The giant welcomed him kindly and led him to a room where there was a good bed.

Tired as he was, Jack could not go to sleep. Soon he heard the giant walking about in the next room and repeating to himself:

> "Though here with me you lodge tonight,
> You shall not see the morning light;
> My club shall dash your brains outright."

"We'll see about that," said Jack to himself. He got out of bed and groped round the dark room. In the fireplace he found a log. He put the log in the bed and hid himself in a corner.

Soon the door opened and the two-headed giant came in. "I'll make short work of you," he said, and he brought down his club upon Jack's pillow. "Now I've battered his brains," the giant muttered and left the room satisfied.

The next morning, Jack walked into the room where the giant sat at breakfast. Of course the giant could hardly believe his four eyes when he saw him, but he pretended not to be surprised.

"I hope you slept well," he said.

"Pretty well, thank you," answered Jack. "I was disturbed a little. Perhaps there were rats in the room. Certainly I heard something."

The giant was very puzzled. How could he have delivered that blow with his club, and yet not have killed Jack? That was a question he could not answer, but he hoped to find out.

Jack was right in thinking he might be invited to breakfast. He had fastened a leather bag beneath his coat, for he supposed the giant would expect him to eat a good deal. He sat opposite his host, who helped him to a large plateful of hasty pudding, then another, and another.

Now Jack ate very little and put most of the pudding into his leather bag when the giant was not looking.

After breakfast Jack said to the giant, "Can you cut yourself open without harm?" and he ripped open the leather bag with a knife, and the pudding fell out.

The giant did not like to be outdone, so he said, "Of course I can cut myself open, if you can." With these words, he plunged his knife into himself and fell down dead. And so it was that Jack became the possessor of the wonderful coat, the remarkable cap, the amazing sword, and the fantastic shoes.

Once more Jack started on his travels, and once more he reached a lonely castle and asked for a night's lodging. This time he was welcomed by many knights and ladies, who invited him to have supper with them. It was a merry company and Jack was enjoying himself thoroughly when a messenger rushed in to say that a two-headed giant was on his way to the castle.

Now this castle was surrounded by a deep moat. To reach it or to leave the moat had to be crossed by going over a drawbridge. Jack quickly set men to work to saw the drawbridge nearly through, so that it could bear no heavy weight. Next he put on his wonderful coat that made him invisible, and his fantastic shoes that could carry him as fast as the wind. Then he crossed the bridge to meet the giant, carrying in his hand the amazing sword that could cut through anything.

The giant could not see Jack because he wore his invisible coat. But he sniffed the air, and sang in a loud voice:

> "Fe, fi, fo, fum,
>
> I smell the blood of an Englishman;
>
> Be he alive, or be he dead,
>
> I'll grind his bones to make my bread."

"Oh, will you indeed. You must catch me first," said Jack. Then throwing off his coat, he ran before the giant, and every now and again he all but let himself be caught. Then he made good use of his shoes of swiftness and in a moment was beyond reach. The giant grew more and more furious as he chased Jack all around the castle.

The lords and ladies watched the chase from one of the towers. They clapped their hands with delight as they saw Jack lead the giant such a dance.

At last Jack crossed the drawbridge. The giant followed, but beneath his heavy weight the sawn bridge snapped and he was hurled headlong into the moat below. Jack now stood on the edge of the moat, laughing.

"I thought you were going to grind my bones to make your bread, eh?" asked Jack.

The giant foamed with rage, but could say nothing.

Then Jack ordered a strong rope to be brought. He threw it over the two heads of the giant, and with the help of a team of horses dragged him to the edge of the moat. Next Jack drew his magic sword and cut off both heads.

Ringing cheers of "Long live Jack the Giant-Killer!" echoed through the castle.

After spending some time with the knights and ladies, Jack set out on his last adventure. He went over hills and dales without meeting anyone. Finally, he came to a little hut at the foot of a high mountain. Jack knocked at the door. It was opened by an old man with hair as white as snow.

"I have lost my way, good father," said Jack. "I wonder if you can give me a night's lodging."

"Come in," said the old man, "if you can be content with humble fare."

Jack said he would be grateful for a meal of any kind, and gladly ate the bread and fruit which were set before him.

After supper the old man said solemnly, "A task lies before you, my son, for your belt tells me that you are Jack the Giant-Killer. At the top of this mountain is an enchanted castle. It belongs to a giant called Galligantus. He, with the help of a magician, changes into a beast each knight and fair lady who approaches his castle, and those who are not so changed are devoured by two fiery dragons which guard the gates. But, worse still, some time ago Galligantus and the magician strolled into the garden of a duke who lives in a neighboring valley. There they saw the duke's beautiful daughter gathering honeysuckle flowers. The magician spoke a magic word, and instantly a chariot, drawn by the two fiery dragons, appeared in the garden. The giant seized the lady, placed her in the chariot, and the dragons drew her through the air to the enchanted castle. There she was changed into a deer, and a deer she must remain until the enchantment is broken. This is the task that lies before you, my son."

"And I go to it gladly," said Jack.

The next morning Jack put on his remarkable cap, his wonderful coat, his fantastic shoes, and carried his amazing sword. Then he wished himself at the castle gate. He was there in a moment, but because of his invisible coat the fiery dragons did not see him. On the gate hung a golden trumpet. Under it were written these words:

>Whoever can this trumpet blow
>Shall cause the giant's overthrow.

As soon as Jack read this, he seized the trumpet and blew a shrill blast. The gates at once flew open and Jack entered the castle.

The giant and the magician were speechless, and unable to move, for they knew that the blast of the golden horn heralded their doom.

Jack lost no time in drawing his magic sword and in a moment the giant Galligantus lay dead before him. Just as he fell, a whirlwind rushed through the castle, carrying away the magician. And a moment later all the birds and beasts in the castle became the knights and ladies that they had been before, and the sad-looking deer was again the duke's beautiful daughter who had been gathering honeysuckle flowers in her father's garden.

Then all the knights and ladies and the duke's daughter and Jack came bounding down the mountainside in delight. When they looked around, the castle had vanished.

At the foot of the mountain, the old man welcomed them joyfully. After he had given them refreshment, they all traveled together to the court of the king. There Jack told of his wonderful adventures with Cormoran, with Blunderbore, with the two-headed giant who killed himself, with the two-headed giant who fell into the moat, and with Galligantus.

Jack's fame soon spread through the whole country and not long afterward the duke said to him, "I should like you to marry my daughter." Since this was what Jack wanted to do more than anything in the world, he was very happy. For the rest of his life he lived in peace, although he was always known far and wide as Jack the Giant-Killer.

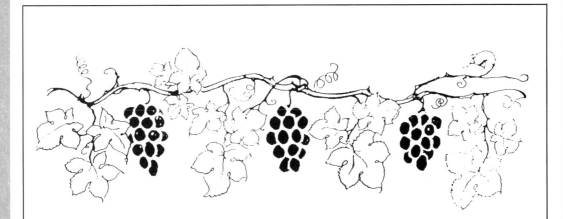

The Fox and the Grapes

A hungry fox saw some fine bunches of grapes hanging from a vine that was trained along a high trellis, and did his best to reach them by jumping as high as he could into the air. But it was all in vain, for they were just out of reach. So he gave up trying and walked away with an air of dignity and unconcern, remarking, "I thought those grapes were ripe, but I see now they are quite sour."

AESOP

The Ugly Duckling

 T was summertime, and it was beautiful in the country. The sunshine fell warmly on an old house, surrounded by deep canals, and from the walls down to the water's edge there grew large burdock leaves, so high that children could stand upright among them without being seen. This place was as wild and lonely as the thickest part of the woods, and it was here that a duck had chosen to make her nest. She was sitting on her eggs; but the pleasure she had felt at first was now almost gone, because she had been there so long.

At last, however, the eggs began to crack, and one little head after another appeared. "Quack, quack!" said the mother duck, and all the little ones got up as well as they could and peeped about from under the green leaves.

"How large the world is!" said one of the ducklings.

"Do you think this is the whole of the world?" asked the mother. "It stretches far away beyond the other side of the garden, down to the pastor's field, but I have never been there. Are you all here?" And then she got up. "No, I have not got you all. The largest egg is still here. How long, I wonder, will this last? I am so weary of it!" And she sat down again.

At last the great egg burst. "Peep, peep!" said the little one, and out it tumbled. But oh! how large and gray and ugly it was! The mother duck looked at it. "That is a great, strong creature," said she. "None of the others is at all like it."

The next day the weather was delightful and the sun was shining warmly when the mother duck with her family went down to the canal. Splash! She went into the water. "Quack, quack!" she cried, and one duckling after another jumped in. The water closed over their heads, but all came up again and swam quite easily. All were there, even the ugly gray one was swimming about with the rest.

"Quack, quack!" said the mother duck. "Now come with me. I will take you into the world. But keep close to me, or someone may step on you. And beware of the cat."

When they came into the duckyard, two families were quarreling about the head of an eel, which in the end was carried off by the cat.

"See, my children, such is the way of the world," said the mother duck, sighing, for she, too, was fond of roasted eels. "Now use your legs," said she, "keep together, and bow to the old duck you see yonder. She is the noblest born of them all, and is of Spanish blood, which accounts for her dignified appearance and manners. And look, she has a red rag on her leg. That is considered a special mark of distinction and is the greatest honor a duck can have."

The other ducks who were in the yard looked at the little family and one of them said aloud, "Only see! Now we have another brood, as if there were not enough of us already. How ugly that one is. We will not endure it." And immediately one of the drakes flew at the poor gray youngster and bit him on the neck.

"Leave him alone," said the mother. "He is doing no one any harm."

"Yes, but he is so large and ungainly."

"Those are fine children that our good mother has," said the old duck with the red rag on her leg. "All are pretty except that one, who certainly is not at all well-favored. I wish his mother could improve him a little."

"Certainly he is not handsome," said the mother, "but he is very good and swims as well as the others, indeed rather better. I think in time he will grow like the others and perhaps will look smaller." And she stroked the duckling's neck and smoothed his ruffled feathers. "Besides," she added, "he is a drake. I think he will be very strong so he will fight his way through."

"The other ducks are very pretty," said the old duck. "Pray make yourselves at home, and if you find an eel's head you can bring it to me."

And accordingly they made themselves at home.

But the poor duckling who had come last out of his eggshell, and who was

so ugly, was bitten, pecked, and teased by both ducks and hens. And the turkey cock, who had come into the world with spurs on, and therefore fancied he was an emperor, puffed himself up like a ship in full sail and quite red with passion marched up to the duckling. The poor thing scarcely knew what to do. He was quite distressed because he was so ugly.

So passed the first day, and afterward matters grew worse and worse. Even his brothers and sisters behaved unkindly, saying, "May the cat take you, you ugly thing!" The ducks bit him, the hens pecked him, and the girl who fed the poultry kicked him. He ran through the hedge and the little birds in the bushes were frightened and flew away. That is because I am so ugly, thought the duckling, and ran on.

At last he came to a wide moor where some wild ducks lived. There he lay the whole night, feeling very tired and sad. In the morning the wild ducks flew up and then they saw their new companion. "Pray who are you?" they asked. The duckling greeted them as politely as possible.

"You are really very ugly," said one of the wild ducks, "but that does not matter to us if you do not wish to marry into our family."

Poor thing! He had never thought of marrying. He only wished to lie among the reeds and drink the water of the moor. There he stayed for two whole days. On the third day along came two wild geese, or rather goslings, for they had not been long out of their eggshells, which accounts for their impertinence.

"Hark ye," they said, "you are so ugly that we like you very well. Will you go with us and become a bird of passage? On another moor, not far from this, are some dear, sweet wild geese, as lovely creatures as have ever said 'hiss, hiss.' It is a chance for you to get a wife. You may be lucky, ugly as you are."

Just then a gun went off and both goslings lay dead among the reeds. Bang! Another gun went off and whole flocks of wild geese flew up from the rushes. Again and again the same alarming noise was heard.

There was a great shooting party. The sportsmen lay in ambush all around. The dogs splashed about in the mud, bending the reeds and rushes in all directions. How frightened the poor little duck was! He turned away his head, thinking to hide it under his wing, and at the same moment a fierce-looking dog passed close to him, his tongue hanging out of his mouth, his eyes sparkling fearfully. His jaws were wide open. He thrust his nose close to the duckling, showing his sharp white teeth, and then he was gone—gone without hurting him.

"Well! Let me be thankful," sighed the duckling. "I am so ugly that even a dog will not bite me."

And he lay still, though the shooting continued among the reeds. The noise did not cease until late in the day, and even then the poor little thing dared not stir. He waited several hours before he looked around him, and then, although it had gotten very windy and was starting to rain, he hastened away from the moor as fast as he could.

Toward evening he reached a little hut, so wretched that he knew not on which side to fall and therefore remained standing. He noticed that the door had lost one of its hinges and hung so much awry that there was a space between it and the wall wide enough to let him through. Since the storm was becoming worse and worse, he crept into the room and hid in a corner.

In this room lived an old woman with her tomcat and her hen. The cat, whom she called her little son, knew how to set up his back and purr. He could even throw out sparks when his fur was stroked the wrong way. The hen had very short legs, and was therefore called Chickie Shortlegs. She laid very good eggs and the old woman loved her as her own child.

The next morning the cat began to mew and the hen to cackle when they saw the new guest.

"What is the matter?" asked the old woman, looking around. Her eyes were not good, so she took the duckling to be a fat duck who had lost her way. "This is a wonderful catch," she said. "I shall now have duck's eggs, if it be not a drake. We must wait and see." So the duckling was kept on trial for three weeks. But no eggs made their appearance.

Day after day the duckling sat in a corner feeling very sad, until finally the fresh air and bright sunshine that came into the room through the open door gave him such a strong desire to swim that he could not help telling the hen.

"What ails you?" said the hen. "You have nothing to do, and therefore you brood over these fancies. Either lay eggs or purr, then you will forget them."

"But it is so delicious to swim," said the duckling, "so delicious when the waters close over your head and you plunge to the bottom."

"Well, that is a queer sort of pleasure," said the hen. "I think you must be crazy. Not to speak of myself, ask the cat—he is the wisest creature I know—whether he would like to swim, or to plunge to the bottom of the water. Ask your mistress. No one is cleverer than she. Do you think she would take pleasure in swimming, and in the waters closing over her head?"

"You do not understand me," said the duckling.

"What! We do not understand you! So you think yourself wiser than the cat and the old woman, not to speak of myself! Do not fancy any such thing, child, but be thankful for all the kindness that has been shown you. Are you not lodged in a warm room, and have you not the advantage of society from which you can learn something? Come, for once take the trouble either to learn to purr or to lay eggs."

"I think I will take my chance and go out into the wide world again," said the duckling.

"Well, go then," said the hen.

So the duckling went away. He soon found water, and swam on the surface and plunged beneath it, but all the other creatures passed him by because of his ugliness. The autumn came. The leaves turned yellow and brown. The wind caught them and danced them about. The air was cold. The clouds were heavy with hail or snow, and the raven sat on the hedge and croaked. The poor duckling was certainly not very comfortable!

One evening, just as the sun was setting, a flock of large birds rose from the brushwood. The duckling had never seen anything so beautiful before. Their plumage was of a dazzling white, and they had long, slender necks. They were swans. They uttered a singular cry, spread out their long, splendid wings, and flew away from these cold regions to warmer countries across the sea. They flew so high, so very high! The ugly duckling's feelings were very strange. He turned round and round in the water like a wheel, strained his neck to look after them, and sent forth such a loud and strange cry that he almost frightened himself.

He could not forget them, those noble birds! Those happy birds! The duckling did not know what the birds were called, or where they were flying, yet he loved them as he had never before loved anything. He did not envy them. It would never have occurred to him to wish such beauty for himself.

He would have been quite content if the ducks in the duckyard had just endured his company.

And the winter was so cold! The duckling had to swim round and round in the water to keep it from freezing. But every night the opening in which he swam became smaller and the duckling had to make good use of his legs to prevent the water from freezing entirely. At last, exhausted, he lay stiff and cold in the ice.

Early in the morning a peasant passed by and saw him. He broke the ice in pieces with his wooden shoe and carried the duckling home to his wife.

The duckling soon revived. The children would have played with him, but he thought they wished to tease him and in his terror jumped into the milk pail, so that the milk was splashed about the room. The good woman screamed and clapped her hands. He flew next into the tub where the butter was kept and then into the meal barrel and out again.

The woman screamed. The children tried to catch him and laughed and screamed, too. It was well for him that the door stood open. He jumped out among the bushes, into the newfallen snow, and lay there as in a dream.

But it would be too sad to relate all the trouble and misery he had to suffer during that winter. He was lying on a moor among the reeds when the sun began to shine warmly again. The larks were singing and beautiful spring had returned.

Once more he shook his wings. They were stronger and carried him forward quickly. And, before he was well aware of it, he was in a large garden where the apple trees stood in full bloom, where the syringas sent forth their fragrance, and hung their long green branches down into the winding canal. Oh! Everything was so lovely, so full of the freshness of spring!

Out of the thicket came three beautiful white swans. They displayed their feathers so proudly, and swam so lightly! The duckling knew the glorious creatures and was seized with a strange sadness.

"I will fly to them, those kingly birds!" he said. "They will kill me, because I, ugly as I am, have presumed to approach them. But it does not matter.

Better be killed by them than be bitten by the ducks, pecked by the hens, kicked by the girl who feeds the poultry, and have so much to suffer during the winter!" He flew into the water and swam toward the beautiful creatures. They saw him and shot forward to meet him. "Only kill me," said the poor duckling and he bowed his head low, expecting death. But what did he see in the water? He saw beneath him his own form, no longer that of a plump, ugly, gray bird. It was the reflection of a swan!

It does not matter to have been born in a duckyard if one has been hatched from a swan's egg.

The larger swans swam around him and stroked him with their beaks. He was very happy.

Some little children were running about in the garden. They threw grain and bread into the water, and the youngest exclaimed, "There is a new one!" The others also cried out, "Yes, a new swan has come!" and they clapped their hands, and ran and told their father and mother. Bread and cake were thrown into the water, and everyone said, "The new one is the best, so young and so beautiful!" and the old swans bowed before him. The young swan felt quite ashamed and hid his head under his wing.

He remembered how he had been laughed at and cruelly treated, and he now heard everyone say he was the most beautiful of all beautiful birds. The syringas bent down their branches toward him, and the sun shone warmly and brightly. He shook his feathers, stretched his slender neck, and in the joy of his heart said, "How little did I dream of so much happiness when I was the ugly, despised duckling!"

FLORENCE CHOATE

Bring the comb and play upon it!
   Marching, here we come!
Willie cocks his highland bonnet,
   Johnnie beats the drum.

Mary Jane commands the party,
   Peter leads the rear;
Feet in time, alert and hearty,
   Each a Grenadier!

All in the most martial manner
   Marching double-quick;
While the napkin like a banner
   Waves upon the stick!

Here's enough of fame and pillage,
   Great commander Jane!
Now that we've been round the village,
   Let's go home again.
               ROBERT LOUIS STEVENSON

WHERE GO THE BOATS?

Dark brown is the river,
   Golden is the sand.
It flows along forever,
   With trees on either hand.

Green leaves a-floating,
   Castles of the foam,
Boats of mine a-boating—
   Where will all come home?

On goes the river
   And out past the mill,
Away down the valley,
   Away down the hill.

Away down the river,
   A hundred miles or more,
Other little children
   Shall bring my boats ashore.
   ROBERT LOUIS STEVENSON

33

Florence Choate

Puss in Boots

HERE was once a miller who, when he died, had nothing to leave to his three sons but a mill, a donkey, and a cat. The mill he left to his eldest son, the donkey to the second, and to the youngest he left the cat.

The youngest son was very unhappy. "Alas!" he said, "This cat is of no use to me and I am too poor to feed her."

"Do not grieve, dear master," said the cat. "You have only to give me a bag and get a pair of boots made for me, so that I may scamper through the dirt and brambles, and you shall find that you are not so badly off as you think."

Now this surprised the miller's son very much, and he thought to himself, A cat that can speak is perhaps wonderful enough to do as she promises. So he brought her the bag and had the boots made for her.

Puss put on the boots with a proud air, slung the bag over her shoulder, and went to the garden. There she gathered some lettuces and put them into the bag. Next she went across the field until she came to a rabbit hole. Then she lay down as if dead, leaving the top of her bag open. A plump rabbit soon peeped out of the hole and, smelling the lettuce, came nearer. It was too tempting. The rabbit's head followed his nose into the bag. The cat quickly pulled the strings and the rabbit was dead.

Proud of her prey, Puss marched with it to the palace and asked to see the king. She was brought before the throne and there, with a low bow, Puss said, "Sire, pray accept this rabbit as a gift from my lord the Marquis of

Carrabas, who commanded me to present it to Your Majesty with the assurance of his respect."

"Tell your master," said the king, "that I accept his gift and am much obliged. "

A few days later, Puss again went to the field. Again she lay down as if dead with her sack open beside her. This time she captured two fine partridges. Again the cat went to the king and presented the partridges as she had done the rabbit. They, too, were accepted, and the king was so pleased that he ordered the cat to be taken to the kitchen and fed. In this manner,

at least once a week, the cat continued to take presents of game to the king from the Marquis of Carrabas.

One day, Puss heard that the king and his beautiful daughter were going to drive along the riverside. The daughter was said to be the most beautiful princess in the world.

"My master," said the cat to the miller's son, "if you will do as I tell you, your fortune is made."

"What would you have me do?" asked the miller's son.

"Only this, dear master. Bathe in the river at a spot I shall show you and believe that you are not yourself but the Marquis of Carrabas."

The miller's son was in a gloomy mood, and did not mind much what he did, so he answered, "Very well, Puss." He went to the river and while he was bathing, the king and all his court passed by and were startled by the cry, "Help, help! My Lord the Marquis of Carrabas is drowning!"

When the king put his head out of the carriage, he saw the cat who had brought him so many presents. He ordered his attendants to go to the assistance of the Marquis of Carrabas. While they were dragging the marquis out of the water, the cat ran to the king, made a low bow, and said, "Your Majesty, what shall my poor master do, for a thief has stolen his clothes?" Now the truth was that the cunning cat had hidden the clothes under a large stone.

"That is most unfortunate," said the king, and he gave orders to a servant to fetch a suit from the castle.

When the miller's son was dressed in the fine clothes he looked like a gentleman, and very handsome. The princess was taken with his appearance, and the Marquis of Carrabas had no sooner cast upon her two or three respectful glances than she fell in love with him. The king insisted that he get into the carriage and take a ride with them.

The cat ran on ahead of the carriage and, reaching a meadow where mowers were cutting the grass, he said to them, "Unless you tell the king when he asks you that these meadows belong to the Marquis of Carrabas, you shall be chopped as fine as mincemeat."

When the king drove by and asked the mowers who owned the meadows they answered, trembling, "They belong to the Marquis of Carrabas, Your Majesty." The king then turned to the miller's son and said, "You indeed own fine meadows, my lord."

Meantime, Puss had run on farther and reached a cornfield in which there were reapers busy at work. "Now, if the king drives by," said the cat to the reapers, "and inquires to whom these fields belong, you must say that they are the property of the Marquis of Carrabas. If you do not, you shall be chopped as fine as mincemeat." So when the king drove by and asked whose fields these were, the frightened reapers answered, "They belong to the Marquis of Carrabas, Your Majesty. "

"What a rich man he must be and how handsome he looks!" said the king to himself as he looked at the miller's son. "I do believe he would be a good husband for my daughter."

Now the fields really belonged to an ogre who lived in a castle a little farther on. When the cat reached the castle she knocked at the door, which was opened by the ogre himself.

"Sir," said Puss, "I am on a journey, and since I have often heard how wonderful you are, I have taken the liberty to call to see you."

"Come in," said the ogre, who was always pleased to be thought wonderful.

"I have heard," continued Puss, "that you can change into any animal you like."

"I can," said the ogre and he instantly changed into a lion. The cat got such a fright that she ran up the wall nearly to the ceiling. But the ogre at once became an ogre again, and the cat jumped down.

"Sir, you really frightened me. But you must admit that it is not so wonderful for such a big gentleman to change into a big animal as it would be if he could change into a little one. I suppose you could not, for instance, change into a mouse."

PUSS IN BOOTS

"Could not?" cried the ogre. "You shall see." And in a moment Puss saw a little brown mouse running about the floor. With one spring she pounced upon it and gobbled it up. And that was the end of the ogre.

By this time the king had arrived at the castle. Puss, hearing the carriage wheels, ran to the gate and cried, "Welcome, Your Majesty, to the castle of the Marquis of Carrabas!"

"What, my lord!" cried the king, turning to the miller's son, "Does this castle also belong to you? I have nothing so fine in my whole kingdom."

The miller's son did not speak, but gave his hand to the princess to help her to alight from the carriage. They entered the castle and, in the dining hall, found preparations for a grand feast, which the ogre had planned to serve to some guests he had expected. But the ogre's friends did not arrive, since news reached them that the king was in the castle.

Every moment the king became more and more charmed with the miller's son. After they had feasted he said, "There is no one in the world I should like so much to be my son-in-law. I now create you a prince."

Then the prince said there was no one in the world he would like so much for his wife as the princess. And the princess said there was no one in the world she would like so much for a husband as the prince. So the two were married and lived happily ever after in the ogre's castle.

And Puss was made a lady-in-waiting. She was the greatest favorite with the king and the prince and the princess. Never again did she have to hunt mice for a meal, but she was served all kinds of delicacies until the end of her days.

The Wolf and the Crane

A wolf once got a bone stuck in his throat. So he went to a crane and begged her to put her long bill down his throat and pull it out. "I'll make it worth your while," he added.

The crane did as she was asked, and got the bone out quite easily. The wolf thanked her warmly and was just turning away, when she cried, "What about that fee of mine?"

"Well, what about it?" snapped the wolf, baring his teeth as he spoke; "you can go about boasting that you once put your head into a wolf's mouth and didn't get it bitten off. What more do you want?"

AESOP

The Dog and the Shadow

A dog was crossing a plank bridge over a stream with a piece of meat in his mouth when he happened to see his own reflection in the water. He thought it was another dog with a piece of meat twice as big, so he let go his own and flew at the other dog to get the larger piece. But, of course, all that happened was that he got neither, for one was only a shadow and the other was carried away by the current.

Aesop

FLORENCE CHOATE

Rumpelstiltskin

NCE a poor miller, who had a very beautiful daughter, was sent for by the king. The miller, who had never in his life been at court, did not feel at all at ease. So, instead of saying something sensible, or keeping quiet, he said to the king, "I have a daughter who can spin gold out of straw." Then the miller thought he had spoken words that would make the king think him an important person.

"Your daughter is indeed clever if she can do as you say," answered the king. "Bring her to my castle tomorrow and we shall see."

So the next day the miller's daughter, dressed in a satin skirt and a velvet bodice, was brought to court. She was at once led to a room which was full of straw. Nothing else was in the room but a spinning wheel. "Now set to work," said the king, "and if between tonight and tomorrow at dawn you have not spun this straw into gold, you must die." Then he went out, carefully locking the door behind him.

So there sat the poor miller's beautiful daughter, knowing not what to do, for she had no idea in the world how to spin straw into gold. She could only hide her face in her hands and weep. Suddenly the locked door sprang open, and in stepped the queerest-looking little man imaginable. His coat and loose trousers were made of white cotton, with large red dots. On his head he wore a red and white hat with a cock's feather. In his right hand he held a wand.

"Good evening, Mistress Miller. But wherefore do you weep?"

"Alas!" answered the maiden. "I have to spin gold out of straw and I know not how to do it."

"But I do," said the little man. "What will you give me if I spin it for you?"

"My necklace," said the miller's daughter.

The little man took the necklace and sat down before the spinning wheel. He spun, and he spun, and he spun, until all the straw had disappeared and all the spindles were filled with gold. Then with a low bow he vanished.

At sunrise the king came, and was astonished to see so much gold. But it only made him want still more. So he took the miller's daughter to a larger room, full of straw, and again he said, "Now set to work, and if, between tonight and tomorrow at dawn, you have not spun this straw into gold, you must die."

When the maiden was left alone she again began to weep in despair. But in a moment the door flew open and again the curious little man stood before her.

"What will you give me if I spin this straw into gold?"

"My ring," said the miller's daughter.

The little man took the ring, and sat down before the spinning wheel. He spun, and he spun, and he spun, until all the straw had disappeared and all the spindles were filled with gold. Then with a low bow the little man again disappeared.

When, in the early morning, the king came, he was delighted to see the shining gold, but he was not yet satisfied. So he led the miller's daughter to a still larger room, full of straw, and this time he said, "Spin this into gold and you shall be my queen. I shall come again at sunrise." Then he left her.

Before long the curious little man again appeared and he once more found the maiden weeping.

"What will you give me if I spin this straw into gold?"

"Alas, I have nothing more that I can give!" said the miller's daughter.

"Then promise me your first child if you become queen," said the little man.

I may never have a little child, thought the girl, and so she promised.

Then the little man sat down before the spindle, and he spun, and he spun, and he spun, until all the straw had disappeared and all the spindles were filled with gold. Then with his usual low bow the strange little man vanished.

When the king came in the morning, he was not sorry to marry the miller's daughter. For even if she be of humble birth, he thought, I could not find a lovelier woman in the world. So the wedding took place that same day.

About a year afterward, the king and queen had a beautiful child. The queen had quite forgotten her promise to the little man and was very happy, when suddenly he entered her room and demanded the baby. The poor queen held her little one tight and said she would part with all the riches of her kingdom if only she might keep the child.

"No," he said, "a human child is dearer to me than all the kingdoms in the world."

Then the poor mother wept as if her heart would break. Finally, the little man took pity on her, and said, "I will give you three days and if in that time you can find out my name, you shall keep your child."

The queen lay awake all night, thinking of all the odd names she had ever heard. The next day the little man came again, and the queen repeated all the names she could remember beginning with Timothy, Benjamin, and Jeremiah. But the little man said, "No, I am not called by any of these."

The next morning the queen sent a messenger all through the kingdom collecting all the names he could find. When the little man came the second time, she tried all sorts of strange names, like Brownbones, Dickybird, and Spindleshanks. But he only shook his head and kept repeating, "No, that's not my name.

On the third day the messenger came back late. "I have not been able to find any new names," said he, "but as I came round the corner of a wood, at the foot of a high mountain, this is what I saw and heard. Close by, there was a little house. In front of it was a fire burning, and round the fire a ridiculous little man was hopping on one leg and singing—

> 'Although today I brew and bake,
> Tomorrow the Queen's own child I take.
> So nobody tell, for goodness' sake,
> That my name is Rumplestiltskin.'"

Oh, how joyful the queen was when she heard this!

Soon the little man came in, made a low bow, and said, "Your Majesty, what is my name?"

The queen was now merry enough to be mischievous, so, instead of saying his real name at once, she asked, "Is it Fred?"

"No."

"Is it Arnold?"

"No."

"Is is Harry?"

"No."

"Is it Henry?"

"No."

"Then it is Rumplestiltskin," cried the queen.

When the little man heard this, he flew into a terrible rage and stamped his foot on the ground so violently that it sank deep into the ground. Then, wild with fury, he seized his left leg with both hands and pulled and pulled. He pulled with such force that his right leg came off. Then Rumplestiltskin hopped away and was never heard of again.

The Children's Hour

Between the dark and the daylight,
   When the night is beginning to lower,
Comes a pause in the day's occupations,
   That is known as the children's hour.

I hear in the chamber above me
   The patter of little feet,
The sound of a door that is opened,
   And voices soft and sweet.

From my study I see in the lamplight,
   Descending the broad hall stair,
Grave Alice, and laughing Allegra,
   And Edith with golden hair.

A whisper, and then a silence:
   Yet I know by their merry eyes
They are plotting and planning together
   To take me by surprise.

A sudden rush from the stairway,
   A sudden raid from the hall!
By three doors left unguarded
   They enter my castle wall!

They climb up into my turret
    O'er the arms and back of my chair;
If I try to escape, they surround me;
    They seem to be everywhere.

They almost devour me with kisses,
    Their arms about me entwine,
Till I think of the Bishop of Bingen
    In his Mouse-Tower on the Rhine!

Do you think, O blue-eyed banditti,
    Because you have scaled the wall,
Such an old mustache as I am
    Is not a match for you all!

I have you fast in my fortess,
    And will not let you depart,
But put you down into the dungeon
    In the round-tower of my heart.

And there will I keep you forever,
    Yes, forever and a day.
Till the walls shall crumble to ruin,
    And moulder in dust away!
    HENRY WADSWORTH LONGFELLOW

The Frog Prince

HERE was once a handsome young prince who had the misfortune to offend a wicked fairy. To avenge herself she turned him into an ugly frog and put him into a well.

Now it happened that the well was in the courtyard of a king's palace and on fine days, when the sun shone warmly, the king's youngest daughter sometimes came there to amuse herself by tossing a golden ball high into the air and catching it as it fell. The poor frog watched her running to and fro in the sunshine. He thought she was the prettiest princess he had ever seen.

One day, the princess threw the ball up so high that when she stretched out her hand to catch it the ball bounced on the stones and fell with a splash into the water. She ran to the edge of the well and gazed down. But the golden ball had sunk far, far out of sight. Only a little ring of bubbles showed her where it had disappeared. She began to cry bitterly.

The frog popped his head out of the water. "Don't cry, Princess!" he said. "What will you give me if I bring your ball from the bottom of the well?"

"Oh, I will give you anything I have," replied the princess. "My pretty

pearls, my diamonds—even my crown. Only please bring my ball back to me!"

"I do not want your pearls or your diamonds or your crown," said the frog. "But if you will promise to love me, and let me eat from your plate, and drink out of your cup, and sleep on your bed, I will bring your ball safely back to you."

And the princess promised. For she said to herself, "What a silly frog! As if he could ever get out of the well and walk all the way to the palace! He will never find me."

The frog dove to the bottom of the well and presently came up with the golden ball in his mouth.

The princess had no sooner snatched it from him than she forgot all about her promise and ran back to the palace laughing with joy.

The next day, as she sat at dinner with the king and his courtiers, something came flopping up the great staircase—flip flap, flip flap! And a voice said:

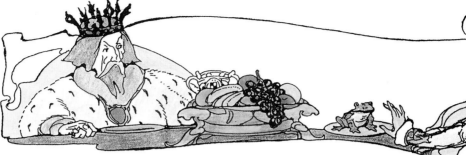

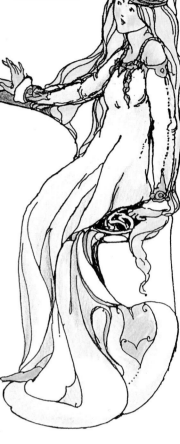

"From the deep and mossy well,
    Little princess, where I dwell,
    When you wept in grief and pain
    I brought your golden ball again."

The princess dropped her spoon with a clatter on her plate, for she knew it was the frog who had come to claim her promise.

"What is the matter, daughter?" asked the king. "There is someone knocking at the door and your rosy cheeks are quite pale."

Then the princess had to tell her father all that had happened the day before—how she had dropped her golden ball into the well, and how the frog had brought it up for her, and of the promises she had given him.

The king frowned and said, "People who make promises must keep them. Open the door and let the frog come in."

The princess opened the door very unwillingly and the poor frog hopped into the room, looking up into her face with his ugly little eyes.

"Lift me up beside you," he cried, "that I may eat from your plate and drink out of your cup." The princess did as he asked her and was obliged to finish her dinner with the frog beside her, for the king sat by to see that she fulfilled her promise. When they had finished, the frog said, "I have had enough to eat. Now I am tired. Take me up and lay me on your pillow, that I may go to sleep."

Then the princess began to cry. It was so dreadful to think that an ugly frog, all cold and damp from the well, should sleep in her pretty white bed. But her father frowned again and said, "People who make promises must keep them. He gave you back your golden ball and you must do as he asks."

So the princess picked the frog up between her thumb and finger, not touching him more than she could help, and carried him upstairs and put him on the pillow on her bed. There he slept all night long. As soon as it was light he jumped up, hopped downstairs, and went out of the palace.

Now, thought the princess, he is gone and I shall be troubled with him no more.

But she was mistaken, for when night came again she heard tapping at the door of her bedroom. When she opened it, the frog came in and slept upon her pillow as before until the morning broke. The third night he did the same. But when the princess awoke the following morning, she was astonished to see, instead of the frog, a handsome prince standing at the head of her bed. He was gazing at her with the most beautiful eyes that ever were seen.

He told her that he had been enchanted by a wicked fairy, who had changed him into the form of a frog, in which he was fated to remain until a princess let him sleep upon her bed for three nights.

"You," said the prince, "have broken this cruel spell and now I have nothing to wish for but that you should go with me to my father's kingdom, where I will marry you and love you as long as you live."

The princess took him to her father and he gave his consent for them to marry. As they spoke a splendid carriage drove up with eight beautiful horses decked with plumes of feathers and golden harness. Behind rode the prince's servant, who had bewailed the misfortune of his dear master so long and so bitterly that his heart had almost burst. Then all set out full of joy for the prince's kingdom. There they arrived safely and lived happily ever after.

A Discovery

Oh! such a funny thing I found
A-crawling slowly on the ground.
Its legs and head and things like that
Were worn just underneath its hat.
And it was much afraid of me
Because, as quick as quick could be,
It pulled its legs in out of sight
And shut its head and tail up tight.

It stayed quite still till mother came
Who said that "Turtle" was its name
And that it lived inside its shell,
Though what it ate she couldn't tell
And laughed because I said a mouse
Would die in such a stuffy house.

ARTHUR ALDEN KNIPE

The Rain Song

It is not raining rain for me,
　　It's raining daffodils;
In every dimpled drop I see
　　Wild flowers on the hills.

The clouds of gray engulf the day
　　And overwhelm the town;
It is not raining rain to me,
　　It's raining roses down.

It is not raining rain to me,
　　But fields of clover bloom,
Where any buccaneering bee
　　May find a bed and room.

A health unto the happy,
　　A fig for him who frets!
It is not raining rain to me,
　　It's raining violets.

　　　　　　　ROBERT LOVERMAN

Dick Whittington and His Cat

LONG, long ago, in England in the reign of the famous King Edward the third, there lived a little boy named Dick Whittington. His father and mother had died when he was very small, so that he remembered nothing at all about them. A kind neighbor had then taken him to raise. All had gone well with him for a year or two, but when this good neighbor died Dick was left a homeless, ragged little fellow running about a country village.

Since poor Dick was not old enough to work, he was very badly off. He got little for his dinner, and sometimes nothing at all for his breakfast, for the people in the village were poor themselves and they could not afford to give him much more than the peelings of the potatoes and, occasionally, a hard crust of bread.

Dick was a bright boy and, wanting to learn a great many things, he was always listening to what everybody talked about. In this way he came to hear many strange things about the great city of London; for at that time many country people thought that London was a wonderful place, where the streets were all paved with gold and there was nothing but music and singing and laughter all the day long.

One day, as Dick was leaning against a signpost, wondering where he might find something to eat, a large wagon and eight horses, all with bells at their heads, drove through the village. Dick thought this wagon must surely be going to the fine city of London, so he asked the driver if he might walk along beside the wagon. When the driver heard that he had no home, and saw how ragged he was, he knew that the little fellow could be no worse off, so he consented. The good-natured people along the road gave Dick food, and at night the driver let him climb into the wagon and sleep on some of the boxes.

And so at last Dick arrived in London. He was in such a hurry to see the fine streets paved with gold that he hardly stopped to thank the kind driver, but ran off as fast as his legs would carry him, through street after street, thinking every moment that he would come to those paved with gold. Dick had seen a golden coin three times in his little village and he remembered what a great many things it would buy. Now, he thought, when he came to the golden streets, he had only to pick up some of the pavement and he would have all the money he could wish for.

Poor little Dick ran until he was tired, and then when it grew dark and he found that, no matter which way he turned, there was nothing but dirt instead of gold, he sat down in a lonely corner and cried himself to sleep.

All night the boy spent in the streets and when morning came, being very hungry, he got up and walked about and asked everybody he met to give him a halfpenny to keep him from starving. At last, a good-natured-looking gentleman saw how hungry he looked.

"Why don't you go to work, my lad?" said he.

"I would," answered Dick, "but I do not know how to get any."

"If you are willing," said the gentleman, "come with me." He took Dick to a hayfield, where he worked briskly and lived merrily until the hay was all made. After this, he found himself as badly off as before.

Several days passed and at last, when he could walk no farther, he laid himself down at the door of a rich merchant, Mr. Fitzwarren. Here he was found by the cook, a cross and mean woman. But before she had a chance to send Dick away, the merchant himself came to the door.

"Why do you lie there, my boy?" he asked. "You seem old enough to be at work."

"But I can find no work," said Dick, "and I am very weak for want of food."

"Poor fellow!" said the merchant. And, being a kindhearted man, he had Dick taken into his home and given a good dinner. Then he told the boy he might stay and help the cook by doing such things as peeling the potatoes, scouring the pots and kettles, and running errands.

Dick would have been very happy in this good family had it not been for the ill-natured cook who always found fault with him and scolded and beat him from morning till night. But although the cook was so ill-tempered, the footman was quite different. An elderly man, he had lived in the family for many years, and was very kindhearted. He felt sorry for the boy and sometimes gave him a halfpenny to buy gingerbread or a top. The footman was fond of reading and often in the evening he would entertain the other servants with some amusing book. Little Dick took pleasure in listening to this good man, which made him wish very much to learn to read, too. So the next time the footman gave him a halfpenny, he bought a little book with it and, with the footman's help, Dick soon learned his letters and afterward to read.

The ill-humored cook was now a little kinder. But Dick had another problem. His bed was in a garret where there were so many holes in the floor and the walls that every night he was awakened by the rats and mice, which made such a noise that he sometimes thought the walls were tumbling down about him. One day, a gentleman who came to see Mr. Fitzwarren required his shoes to be cleaned. Dick took great pains to make them shine and the gentleman gave him a penny. With this Dick decided he would buy a cat. The next day, seeing a little girl with a cat under her arm, he went up to her and asked if she would let him have it for a penny. The girl said she would and told him that the cat was a very good mouser.

Dick kept the cat in the garret, and always took care to carry part of his dinner to her. And in a short time he had no more trouble from the rats and mice.

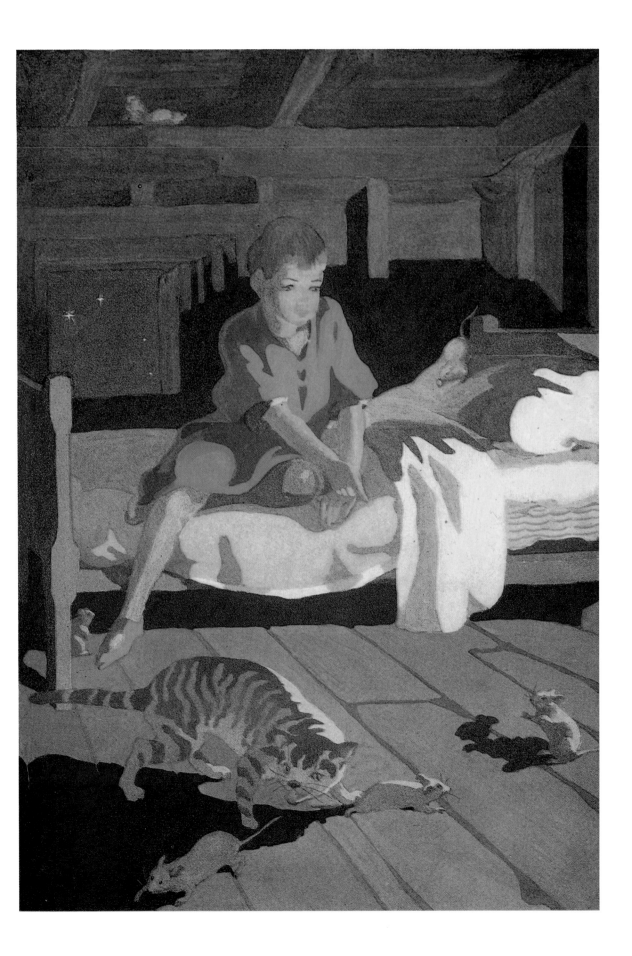

Mr. Fitzwarren was a merchant who filled his ships with all kinds of goods and sent them to foreign countries. Since he was a kind man, he let his servants send anything they wanted to sell.

One of the ships was now ready to sail. Mr. Fitzwarren called all his servants in, and they came, one by one, and left with him the things they wanted to send. They all had something that they were willing to venture, except poor Dick, who had neither money nor goods. For this reason he did not come into the parlor with the rest. But Mr. Fitzwarren ordered him to be called in.

Poor Dick said he had nothing but a cat.

"Why don't you send your cat?" said the merchant's young and pretty daughter, Alice. "You must send something!"

Dick could not bear to part with the faithful mouser, but Alice had always been kind to him and he wished to please her. So the cat was given to the merchant and he laughingly sent it along with his rich cargo.

But Dick missed his cat sorely. The rats and the mice came back to his garret and bothered him so that he could not sleep at night. The cook began to beat and scold him even more than she had done before. It was a hard life for the boy.

At last, when he felt that he could not bear it any longer, he tied his few belongings in a handkerchief and, early one morning, crept out of the house and started to walk back to the little village from which he had come.

He walked as far as Highgate, and there, at a crossroad, he sat down on a stone, which to this day is called Whittington's Stone, and tried to decide on the road he should take. And as he sat there the bells of Bow Church began to ring, and the sound carried far across the fields. Dick thought he heard them say:

> "Turn-a-gain, Whitt-ing-ton,
> Thrice-Lord-Mayor of-Lon-don!"

Lord Mayor of London! he said to himself. They mean for me to take this road.

But scarcely had he taken three steps along the road to the left, when the bells rang once more:

> "Turn-a-gain, Whitt-ing-ton,
> Thrice-Lord-Mayor of-Lon-don!"

So Dick turned and started along the road to the right. But again the bells rang out:

> "Turn-a-gain, Whitt-ing-ton,
> Thrice-Lord-Mayor of-Lon-don!"

After all, thought Dick, it is only the cook who treats me badly. I will turn and go back to the city. What do I care for her scoldings and beatings if some day I am to be Lord Mayor of London!

Dick went back and was lucky enough to get into the house, and set about his work, before the cook even knew he had been gone.

The merchant's ship, with Dick's cat on board, was a long time at sea. But at last it arrived in a country on the coast of Barbary. The people came in great numbers to see the sailors and to buy the fine things with which the ship was laden. The captain, as was his custom on arriving in a foreign country, sent the king some rich presents. The king was so delighted that he invited the captain to the palace to dine with him.

The dining hall was magnificent. The walls were studded with jewels and the carpet was strewn with flowers of gold and silver. The king and queen, in gorgeous robes, welcomed the captain and they sat down to dinner. A number of servants brought in many dishes piled high with rich food. But,

to the amazement of the captain, a vast horde of rats and mice rushed in and ate everything in sight.

"There!" sighed the king. "My dinner is gone again today! I would give half the wealth of my kingdom to get rid of them!"

"Why don't you get a cat?" asked the captain.

"A cat?" said the king. "What is that? Is that a new kind of tiger? I have tried tigers and lions, but not one of them will kill a mouse for me."

The captain, remembering poor Whittington's cat, hurriedly sent a sailor down to the ship to bring it. In the meantime, the king had another dinner prepared. The cat and dinner arrived at about the same time. When the sailor entered the dining hall with the cat in his arms, the table was full of rats and mice. When the cat saw them she did not wait for anybody's bidding, but made one spring into their midst. In a few minutes most of the rats and mice lay dead at her feet and the others had scampered off to their holes.

The king and queen were so delighted to be thus rid of their plague that they bought the captain's whole cargo, and then gave him ten bags of gold for the cat.

And so it was that shortly after Dick returned to London, the merchant's ship reached port and the captain hurried to Mr. Fitzwarren to tell him of his great success and of Dick's good fortune.

"I have ten bags of gold for him," the captain reported.

Mr. Fitzwarren now showed himself a really good man, for while some of his clerks said so great a treasure was too much for such a boy as Dick, he answered, "God forbid that I should keep the value of a single penny from him! It is all his own and he shall have every farthing's worth of it."

He sent for Dick, who happened to be scouring the cook's kettles and was quite dirty, so that he wanted to excuse himself from going to his master. Mr. Fitzwarren, however, made him come in and ordered a chair to be set for him, so that poor Dick thought they were making fun of him.

"Indeed, Mr. Whittington," said the merchant, "we are all in earnest with you. I heartily rejoice in the news these gentlemen have brought you. The captain has sold your cat to the King of Barbary and he has brought you, in return for her, more riches than I possess. I wish you may long enjoy them!"

Mr. Fitzwarren then told the men to give Dick the great treasure they had brought with them, and said, "Mr. Whittington has now nothing to do but to put it in some place of safety."

Dick hardly knew how to behave himself for joy. He begged his master to take what part of the gold he pleased, since he owed it all to his kindness.

"No, no," answered Mr. Fitzwarren, "this is all your own and I have no doubt you will use it well."

Dick next asked his mistress, and then Alice, to accept a part of his good fortune. But they would not, and told him that his success gave them great pleasure. Dick was too kindhearted to keep all the gold for himself. He made

handsome presents to the captain, the mate, and every one of the sailors, and afterward to his good friend the footman and the rest of Mr. Fitzwarren's servants, even to the ill-natured cook. After this, Mr. Fitzwarren advised him to get himself dressed like a gentleman and told him he was welcome to live in his house until he could provide himself with a better home.

When Dick's face was washed, his hair combed, and he was dressed in a nice suit of clothes, he was as handsome as any young man who visited at Mr. Fitzwarren's. Alice, who had always been kind to him, now looked upon him as fit to be her sweetheart; and the more so, no doubt, because Whittington was now always thinking what he could do to please her and giving her the prettiest presents. Mr. Fitzwarren soon became aware of their love for each other and proposed to join them in marriage. To this they both readily agreed. A day for the wedding was soon set and it was attended by the Lord Mayor, the Court of Aldermen, the Sheriffs, and a great number of the richest merchants in London.

History tells us that Dick Whittington and his lady had several children. He was Sheriff of London in the year 1360 and several times afterwards served as Lord Mayor. The last time, he entertained King Henry the fifth on His Majesty's return from the famous Battle of Agincourt. In this company, the king, because of Whittington's gallantry, said, "Never had prince such a subject." When Whittington was told this at the table, he answered, "Never had subject such a king."

Going with an address from the city, on one of the king's victories, he received the honor of knighthood. Sir Richard Whittington supported many poor people. He built a church and also a college, with a yearly allowance to poor scholars, and near it built a hospital.

The Bow Church bells had spoken truly when they chimed:
"Turn-a-gain, Whitt-ing-ton,
Thrice-Lord-Mayor of-Lon-don!"
He and Alice lived happily and in great splendor for many, many years.

Hansel and Gretel

O N on the borders of a dark forest, far away, there once lived a woodcutter with his wife and two children. The woodcutter was very poor indeed, and the children, who were called Hansel and Gretel, had often not enough bread to eat. Their mother had died when they were very little and the woodcutter's new wife did not care for children, so times were hard for Hansel and Gretel.

As winter came on they grew poorer and poorer, until at last one night the poor woodcutter said to his wife, "What are we to do? There is only one loaf of bread left and I fear we shall starve."

"We must get rid of the children," answered his wife. "Tomorrow we will take them into the wood and leave them there. They will never be able to find their way home."

"Oh no!" said the father, "I could not leave them there to starve."

"Well, we shall all starve together if they stay with us," answered his wife, "so it will come to the same thing in the end."

And she talked to her husband until she made him promise to do as she had said.

Now, although it was late, Hansel and Gretel were wide awake, for they were too hungry to sleep, and they could not help hearing all the plans that were made.

"Oh!" sobbed Gretel, "we shall be lost in the dark wood, and the wild beasts will eat us."

"Do not cry, little sister," said Hansel. "I will take care of you." And he slipped out of bed and put on his coat.

Then he softly unbarred the door and stepped out on the garden path. The moon was shining brightly, and the white pebbles on the path shone like new pennies. Hansel stooped down and filled his pockets with as many pebbles as they would hold. Then he went in and crept back into bed again.

The next morning the wife came and woke the children very early. She told them they must get up and dress themselves quickly.

"You shall go with us to the forest today, while your father cuts wood," she said.

Then she gave them each a thick slice of bread for their dinner, and they all set out together. Gretel carried both slices of bread in her apron, for Hansel's pockets were full of pebbles.

Now, as they went along, the father noticed that Hansel stopped and looked back every few minutes.

"Why do you look back so often, my son?" he asked. "If you do not take care you will stumble and fall."

"I only looked back to see my little white cat who is sitting on the roof," answered Hansel. "She wants to say good-bye to me."

"Nonsense!" cried the woodcutter's wife. "There is no cat. It is only the morning sun shining on the wet roof."

But Hansel was not really looking at the cat, for each time he turned around he dropped a white pebble on the road to mark the way which they were taking.

As they went farther and farther into the wood, the road grew more and more difficult. At last the woodcutter stopped and told the children to gather some sticks and make them into a heap.

"I am going to light a fire to warm you," he said, "and then you can rest here until I return."

So Hansel and Gretel sat and warmed themselves at the fire and ate their slices of bread quite happily, for they thought they heard their father chopping wood close by. But the sound they heard was only the dead branch of a tree swinging in the wind. Then, felling very tired after their long walk, they curled themselves up on the dry leaves and fell fast asleep.

When they awoke it was quite dark and the fire was out. The only sound they heard was the hooting of the owls overhead.

"Oh Hansel, what shall we do?" sobbed Gretel. "We are lost in the wood and we shall never be able to find our way home."

"Only wait until the moon rises, little sister," said Hansel. "Give me your hand and I will take you safely home."

And when the moon began to rise and send silver moonbeams to light up the dark forest, the children set out, hand in hand, and found the white pebbles shining like little lamps all the way to the cottage.

"You bad children!" cried the woodcutter's wife, when she opened the door to let them in. "We thought you were never coming home."

But their father took them up in his arms and kissed them over and over again in his joy, for he had been afraid that he would never see them again.

Not long after this there came a day when there was only half a loaf of bread left in the little hut. The wife said to her husband, "We are even poorer than we were before. Must we all starve together or shall we take the children once more to the forest, where they cannot possibly find their way home?"

The woodcutter was very unhappy at the thought, but because he had once said "Yes," it was now twice as difficult to say "No."

The children lay trembling in their beds as they listened to these plans, and poor little Gretel was terribly frightened. But Hansel comforted her again and slipped out of bed to fill his pockets with the white pebbles. This time, however, the door was locked and barred.

Hansel could not get out and he had to creep back to bed again and think of some other plan.

"Come, get up, you lazy children!" cried the wife next morning. "You are going to the forest with us today. Here is your dinner."

And she gave them two small slices of bread.

Gretel put her slice into her pocket, but Hansel crumbled his into small

pieces, and these he dropped along the way as he had done with the pebbles.

"What are you turning round to look at?" asked the woman. "Be quick and do not linger."

"I was only saying good-bye to my white pigeon who is sitting on the roof," said Hansel.

"Nonsense!" cried the woman. "There is no pigeon. It is only the morning sun shining on the wet roof."

But she did not see that every time Hansel stopped to look back he dropped a crumb to mark the way.

This time they went much farther into the heart of the wood. When the children were tired, their father told them to gather wood so he could make them a fire.

"You can rest until we come back," he said.

So they rested by the fire and Gretel shared her slice of bread with Hansel. Then they grew so tired of waiting for their father that they fell fast asleep.

It was quite dark when they woke. Gretel wept, for she was sure there were wild beasts prowling about ready to eat them up. But Hansel was quite brave.

"I will take care of you, little sister," he said. "And I can easily find my way home, for I marked the road with my breadcrumbs."

But alas! The birds had eaten up every crumb and there was not one left to show them the way home. Still they wandered on and on, all that night and all next day, but they only seemed to get deeper and deeper into the forest. They had nothing to eat but a few berries which they found in the wood. When the third day dawned they were nearly starving.

"Oh Hansel!" said Gretel, "I think we shall be obliged to eat the fairy toadstools."

But Hansel held her hand tight and led her on. Suddenly they saw a beautiful white bird sitting on the branch of a tree overhead. It sang so sweetly that the children stopped to listen to it. When it spread its great white fluttering wings and flew off they ran after it as quickly as they could. It seemed to know that the children were following, for it circled slowly in front of them until it stopped over a tiny cottage in the heart of the wood.

And when the children came near they found it was the most wonderful cottage they had ever seen. It was built entirely of gingerbread and ornamented with cookies. The windows were made of transparent candy and the steps of toffee.

"What a feast we shall have!" cried Hansel, standing on tiptoe to break off a piece of the overhanging gingerbread roof. "Help yourself to a pane of candy, little sister, or a step of toffee."

Gretel took a piece of gingerbread in one hand and a pane of hard candy in the other, and sat down on a toffee step to enjoy herself. As they were both eating they heard a gentle voice from the inside of the cottage saying:

"Munching and crunching! Do I hear a mouse
    Eating the walls of my gingerbread house?"

But the children answered quickly—

"'Tis only the wind you mistake for a mouse,
    And no one is eating your gingerbread house."

Then, as the children went on eating, the cottage door opened and an old, old woman hobbled out.

Hansel dropped his square of gingerbread, and Gretel paused with a mouthful of candy. They were both so frightened they could not move.

"Dear little children," said the old woman, "do not be afraid of me. You

are welcome to eat as much of my house as you like. But come inside and I will give you a nice dinner."

Then she led the children in and fed them on pancakes and apple tarts and cream. Afterwards she tucked them into two little white beds. The children felt as if they were in heaven.

But although the old woman seemed so kind and good, she was really a wicked old witch who loved to catch fat little children and kill and eat them. She had red eyes, which didn't see very far, but she could smell things as quickly as a fox, and she knew when Hansel and Gretel were wandering in the forest. She had built the gingerbread house just to catch them.

Early next morning the old witch went in to look at the sleeping children. She rubbed her withered old hands with glee when she saw how tender and fresh they looked. She would have liked them to be plumper, but that was easily mended. So she seized Hansel with her bony hand, and before he was half awake she thrust him into a little iron cage and fastened the grating in front. Then she shook Gretel roughly by the shoulder.

"Get up, you lazy little girl!" she cried. "You must light the fire and fill the big pot with water and help me to make the breakfast. For I have shut

your brother up in a cage and I am going to fatten him until he is plump enough to cook for my supper."

So poor little Gretel was obliged to do as the old witch bade her. And while Hansel was fed on the choicest dainties, she had only shellfish and crabs' claws to eat. And every day the old witch would go to the little iron cage and say to Hansel, "Little boy, put out your finger that I may see how fat you are growing."

Hansel knew that she could not see with her red eyes, so he poked out a bone instead of his finger. And every day when she felt it, she grumbled fearfully because he never seemed to grow fatter.

At last she could wait no longer and she said to Gretel, "You must get up very early tomorrow morning, for there is plenty of work for you to do. I am going to cook your brother for dinner. You must light the fire, heat the oven, and help me prepare for the feast."

Poor Gretel cried as if her heart would break. "Oh, how I wish we had starved together in the wood, or been eaten up by the wild beasts!" she sobbed. "Anything would have been better than this."

"Wishing will not do you much good," said the wicked old witch, blinking her red eyes with glee. "And stop those foolish tears or you will put the fire out."

Gretel went about with a very heavy heart the next day as she lit the fire and filled the big pot with water and heated the great stone oven. And when it was all ready the old witch called to her and said, "I have kneaded the dough and the loaves are ready for baking. Come, little girl, creep into the oven and tell me if it is hot enough."

Now the old witch meant to shut the oven door as soon as the child was inside and bake her for dinner instead of the bread, but Gretel guessed what she meant to do.

"The door is too small and I don't know how to get in," she said.

"What nonsense!" answered the witch. "See! It is quite big enough. You put your head in first, like this.

And the old witch stooped down and poked her head inside the oven.

Quick as thought Gretel ran behind and with all her might gave her a sudden push so that the old witch went headlong into the oven. Gretel banged the door shut and fastened it securely.

Then she found the key of Hansel's cage and ran quickly to let him out.

"The old witch is safe in the oven," she cried, and they threw their arms round each other and danced for joy.

After that they went into the cottage and opened all the witch's treasure chests. Hansel filled his pockets with pearls and diamonds and rubies, while Gretel took as many jewels as her little apron would hold.

Then, hand in hand, they set out once more to try to find their way home, and very glad they were to leave the witch's cottage behind. They had not gone far through the wood when they came to a great lake, so broad that it would be impossible to cross it without a boat.

"What shall we do?" said Hansel. "There is no bridge, and I can see no boat to carry us over."

"Look," said Gretel. "I see a white duck swimming out there. Perhaps she will help us."

And she began to sing:

"Little duck, little duck, help us, we pray.
We are two little children who've quite lost their way.
I know you are kind by your gentle quack, quack.
Will you carry us over upon your white back?"

Then the duck came swimming to her at once, quite ready to carry them across. Hansel climbed onto her back first and wanted Gretel to sit on his knee, but she was afraid they would be too heavy for the kind duck, so she waited until Hansel had crossed to the other side and the duck returned to carry her over, too.

And when they stood together on the opposite shore of the lake they found, to their joy, that it was a part of the wood which they knew quite well. They ran along quickly and at the next turning they came in sight of their own little hut and saw their father standing at the door.

The poor woodcutter was overjoyed when the children rushed into his arms. He had never known a moment's happiness since he had left the children in the wood. And now he was all alone, for his wife had died. He held the children in his arms and cried for joy. They told him all about their adventures and how they had escaped from the wicked witch.

"And see what we have brought home!" said Gretel, opening her apron and showing the glittering jewels.

"And look how full my pockets are!" said Hansel, turning them out, until the floor was covered with precious stones.

Now they had riches enough to last them all their days and they would never be hungry again. But though the diamonds and rubies were very precious, Hansel and Gretel thought they were not half as beautiful as the little white pebbles on the garden walk, which shone brightly when the moon came out and bathed them in silver light.

MY SHIP AND I.

O it's I that am the captain of a tidy little ship,
   Of a ship that goes a-sailing on the pond;
And my ship it keeps a-turning all around and all about;
But when I'm a little older, I shall find the secret out
   How to send my vessel sailing on beyond.

For I mean to grow as little as the dolly at the helm,
   And the dolly I intend to come alive;
And with him beside to help me, it's a-sailing I shall go,
It's a-sailing on the water, when the jolly breezes blow,
   And the vessel goes a divie-divie dive.

O it's then you'll see me sailing through the rushes and the reeds,
   And you'll hear the water singing at the prow;
For beside the dolly sailor, I'm to voyage and explore,
To land upon the island where no dolly was before,
   And to fire the penny cannon in the bow.

ROBERT LOUIS STEVENSON

THE SWING

How do you like to go up in a swing,
    Up in the air so blue?
Oh, I do think it the pleasantest thing
    Ever a child can do!

Up in the air and over the wall,
    Till I can see so wide,
Rivers and trees and cattle and all
    Over the countryside—

Till I look down on the garden green,
    Down on the roof so brown—
Up in the air I go flying again,
    Up in the air and down!

ROBERT LOUIS STEVENSON

Paul Revere's Ride

Listen, my children, and you shall hear
Of the midnight ride of Paul Revere,
On the eighteenth of April, in Seventy-five;
Hardly a man is now alive
Who remembers that famous day and year.

He said to his friend, "If the British march
By land or sea from the town tonight,
Hang a lantern aloft in the belfry-arch
Of the North Church tower as a signal light,—
One, if by land, and two, if by sea;
And I on the opposite shore will be,
Ready to ride and spread the alarm
Through every Middlesex village and farm,
For the country-folk to be up and to arm."

Then he said, "Good night!" and with muffled oar
Silently rowed to the Charlestown shore,
Just as the moon rose over the bay,
Where swinging wide at her moorings lay
The *Somerset*, British man-of-war;
A phantom ship, with each mast and spar
Across the moon like a prison-bar,
And a huge black hulk, that was magnified
By its own reflection in the tide.

Meanwhile, his friend, through alley and street,
Wanders and watches with eager ears,
Till in the silence around him he hears
The muster of men at the barrack-door,
The sound of arms, and the tramp of feet,
And the measured tread of the grenadiers,
Marching down to their boats on the shore.

Then he climbed to the tower of the old North Church,
Up the wooden stairs, with stealthy tread,
To the belfry-chamber overhead,
And startled the pigeons from their perch
On the somber rafters, that round him made
Masses and moving shapes of shade,
Up the trembling ladder, steep and tall,
To the highest window in the wall,
Where he paused to listen and look down
A moment on the roofs of the town,
And the moonlight flowing over all.

Beneath, in the churchyard, by the dead,
In their night encampment on the hill,
Wrapped in silence so deep and still
That he could hear, like a sentinel's tread
The watchful night-wind, as it went
Creeping along from tent to tent,
And seeming to whisper, "All is well!"
A moment only he feels the spell
Of the place and the hour, and the secret dread
Of the lonely belfry and the dead;
For suddenly all his thoughts are bent
On a shadowy something far away,
Where the river widens to meet the bay,—
A line of black that bends and floats
On the rising tide, like a bridge of boats.

Meanwhile, impatient to mount and ride,
Booted and spurred, with a heavy stride
On the opposite shore walked Paul Revere.
Now he patted his horse's side,
Now gazed at the landscape far and near,
Then, impetuous, stamped the earth,
And turned and tightened his saddle-girth;
But mostly he watched with eager search
The belfry tower of the Old North Church,
As it rose above the graves on the hill,
Lonely and spectral, and somber and still.
And lo! as he looks, on the belfry's height
A glimmer, and then a gleam of light!
He springs to the saddle, the bridle he turns,
But lingers and gazes, till full on his sight
A second lamp in the belfry burns!

PAUL REVERE'S RIDE

A hurry of hoofs in a village street,
A shape in the moonlight, a bulk in the dark,
And beneath, from the pebbles, in passing, a spark—
Struck out by a steed flying fearless and fleet!
That was all! And yet, through the gloom and the light
The fate of a nation was riding that night;
And the spark struck out by that steed in his flight,
Kindled the land into flame with its heat.

He has left the village and mounted the steep,
And beneath him, tranquil and broad and deep,
Is the Mystic, meeting the ocean tides;
And under the alders, that skirt its edge,
Now soft in the sand, now loud on the ledge,
Is heard the tramp of his steed as he rides.

It was twelve by the village clock,
When he crossed the bridge into Medford town.
He heard the crowing of the cock,
And the barking of the farmer's dog,
And felt the damp of the river fog,
That rises after the sun goes down.

It was one by the village clock,
When he galloped into Lexington;
He saw the gilded weathercock
Swim in the moonlight as he passed,
And the meeting-house windows, blank and bare,
Gaze at him with a spectral glare,
As if they already stood aghast
At the bloody work they would look upon.

PAUL REVERE'S RIDE

It was two by the village clock,
When he came to the bridge in Concord town.
He heard the bleating of the flock,
And the twitter of birds among the trees,
And felt the breath of the morning breeze
Blowing over the meadows brown.
And one was safe and asleep in his bed
Who at the bridge would be first to fall,
Who that day would be lying dead,
Pierced by a British musket-ball.

You know the rest. In the books you have read,
How the British Regulars fired and fled—
How the farmers gave them ball for ball,
From behind each fence and farmyard wall,
Chasing the redcoats down the lane,
Then crossing the fields to emerge again
Under the trees at the turn of the road,
And only pausing to fire and load.

So through the night rode Paul Revere;
And so through the night went his cry of alarm
To every Middlesex village and farm—
A cry of defiance and not of fear,
A voice in the darkness, a knock at the door,
And a word that shall echo for evermore!
For, borne on the night-wind of the Past,
Through all our history, to the last,
In the hour of darkness and peril and need
The people will waken and listen to hear
The hurrying hoofbeats of that steed,
And the midnight message of Paul Revere.

HENRY WADSWORTH LONGFELLOW

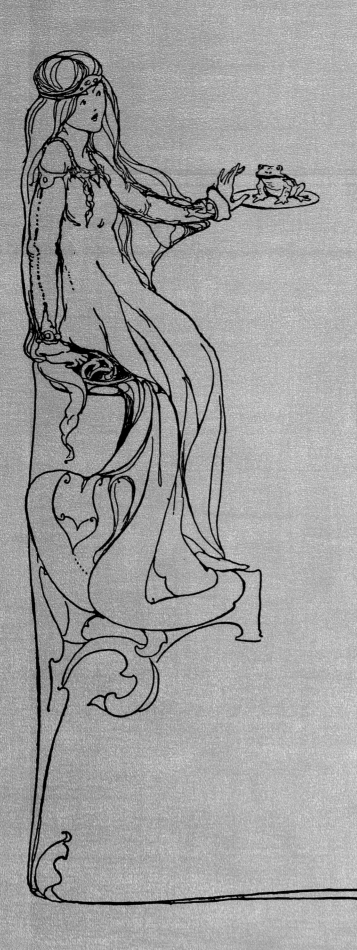